ARNOLD GETS ANGRY

An Emotional Literacy Book

Written by
Lawrence E. Shapiro, Ph.D.
and Illustrated by
Steve Harpster

Arnold Gets Angry
Copyright © 2005 CTC Publishing

Author: Lawrence E. Shapiro, Ph.D.
Illustrator: Steve Harpster
Graphic Design: Chris O'Connor

Summary: *Arnold Gets Angry* teaches children about the causes of their anger, the effect of their anger on others, and how to control and change their angry feelings.

ISBN-10: 0-9747789-0-7
ISBN-13: 978-0-9747789-0-7

Published by:
CTC Publishing
9 North 3rd St. Suite 200Q
Warrenton, VA 20186
Phone: 540-349-1960
Fax: 540-349-1961
Website: www.couragetochange.com

To The Boys and Girls Reading This Book,

My name is Dr. Larry Shapiro, and I'm a child psychologist. Some children call me Dr. Larry.

A child psychologist is someone who helps children with their problems, particularly the problems they have with different feelings.

Many children have problems with their anger. I know some children who seem to be angry all the time. These children are very unhappy and they have a hard time making friends.

I know other children who get angry for the wrong reasons. I know one young man who gets angry at his mother every time he doesn't get what he wants. If she makes something he doesn't like, he gets angry. If she tells him it is bedtime and he wants to stay up, he gets angry. But that doesn't make sense, because we can't have everything just the way we want it all of the time, can we?

Some children I know never get angry, and that isn't good either. Everybody gets angry sometimes and for many different reasons.

I hope this book makes you think about what makes you angry, and how you express your anger. Learning to control your anger is an important part of growing up.

As Arnold and his friends learn about anger, I hope you do, too.

Remember: All feelings are okay. It's what you do with them that counts!

Your friend,
Dr. Larry

Everyone gets angry sometimes.

People look a certain way when they are angry. Can you make a face like you are angry? How do you stand or move your hands when you are angry?

Anger is just one of many feelings that everyone has.

Excited!

Proud

SAD

Happy

calm

ANGRY

depressed

lonely

Jealous

Some people get angry
when they hurt themselves.

Sometimes they blame other people for their problems.

I get angry when the baby pulls my tail. But I would never growl at her. She's just a baby.

Why are you so stupid?

People get angry when things go wrong.

Negative thinking makes things worse.

Everything bad happens to me. This is the worst day of my life.

Most people get angry when someone gets angry at them.

It is okay to be angry.

Sulking makes things worse.

Screaming or crying makes things worse.

Some ways of expressing anger just make things worse.

Stomping, kicking, or hitting things makes things worse.

Being disrespectful makes things worse.

Sometimes you can see why someone is angry at you. A messy room makes most parents angry.

Other times it is hard to understand why someone is so angry.

Many kids get angry
with work that is hard.

Everyone gets angry now and then. But if you are angry a lot, you will feel bad a lot of the time.

Anger can
give you a
headache.

Anger
makes your
muscles
tense.

Anger makes
your heart
beat fast.

Anger makes you
feel bad all over.

Your anger makes other
people feel bad, too.
Angry words hurt
people's feelings.

I don't like it
when people get
mad at me.

25

If you are angry all of the time, it will be hard to have friends.

Kids like other kids
who are happy and
fun to be with.

If you are mad at grown-ups all of the time, they will probably be mad, too.

When something makes you angry you should talk about it.

You can talk to your friends.

You can talk to your parents.

You can talk to your teacher.

You can talk to
a counselor.

When you are angry or upset, you can calm yourself down.

Take 10 deep breaths
and let them out
very slowly.
This will help
make you calm.

There are many ways you can make yourself feel better.

Listening to quiet music or thinking about something peaceful will help relax you.

When you are a good problem-solver you won't be so angry.

You can avoid situations
that might make you angry.

Sometimes you will get angry, even when you don't want to.

Saying you're sorry always helps. Doing something nice for someone is even better!

When Arnold Gets Angry, He Knows What To Do

- Talk about what makes you angry. It really helps.

- Calm yourself down. There are many ways you can make yourself feel better.

- Be a good problem-solver. Then you won't get so angry.

- If you hurt someone with your anger, say you are sorry and do something nice for the person you hurt.

Increasing A Child's Emotional Literacy

Many experts in the fields of mental health and education believe that emotional literacy is as important to a child's school success as traditional academic training. Hundreds of studies have revealed that the people who succeed in life are not always those with good grades and high test scores. In fact, children with good emotional, social, and behavioral skills are more likely to succeed in school and work. They also are more likely to have rewarding friendships and other positive relationships. These children are less likely to have mental health problems or to experiment with drugs and alcohol. Children with good emotional skills are even less likely to have physical health problems as they grow older.

The books in the Emotional Literacy Series are intended to introduce children to the many aspects of their emotional development. Each book in the series is designed to explore a particular emotional or social issue and to get children to think about their behavior. As in any kind of learning, caring and concerned adults can make the difference. Look for opportunities to talk about a child's emotional concerns, and make sure that you are a good role model.

Every book in this series teaches children new emotional skills. We hope that you will take the time to help children practice these skills and praise them when they use them appropriately.

Remember: All feelings are okay. It's what you do with them that counts.